noodles®

I LOVE SCHOOL!

For Gina Shaw,
an editor and friend
without equal

ISBN 978-0-545-13474-3

Copyright © 2009 by Hans Wilhelm, Inc.

All rights reserved. Published by Scholastic Inc.
SCHOLASTIC, CARTWHEEL BOOKS, NOODLES, and associated logos are trademarks and/or registered trademarks of Scholastic Inc.
Lexile is a registered trademark of MetaMetrics, Inc.

Library of Congress Cataloging-in-Publication Data is available.

19   16/0

Printed in the U.S.A.   40
This edition first printing, July 2010

SCHOLASTIC READER
LEVEL 1
50-250 WORDS

I LOVE SCHOOL!

by Hans Wilhelm

Cartwheel
·B·O·O·K·S·®

SCHOLASTIC INC.

New York   Toronto   London   Auckland
Sydney   Mexico City   New Delhi   Hong Kong

School looks like fun.

This must be the way inside.

What a big place!

Where is everyone?

Now I'm totally lost.

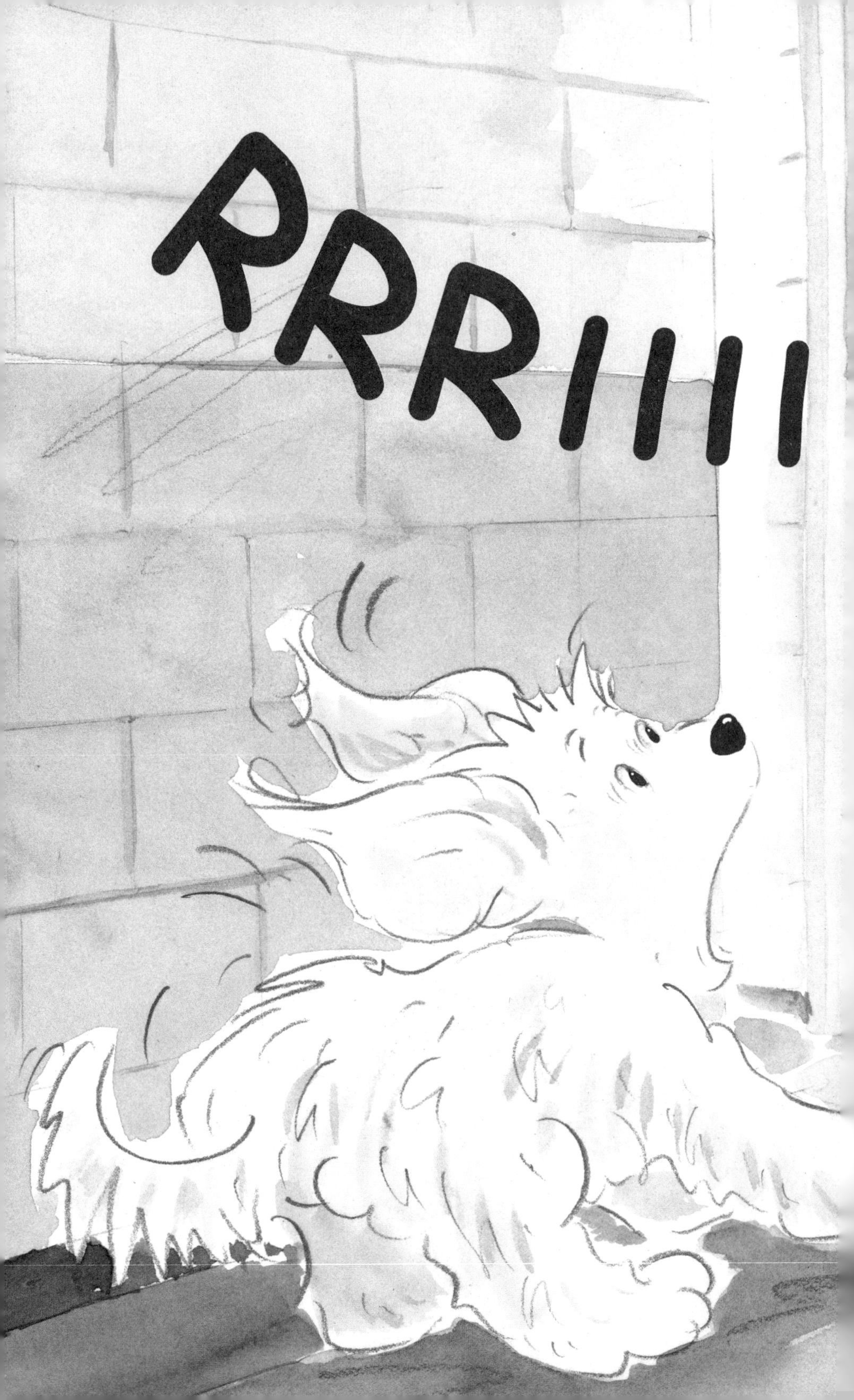
RRRIIIII

INNNGG!

Ahhh!
What is *that*?

I have to get out of here!

I better stay out of the way.

This place is scary.
I feel all alone here.

Wait! That's silly!
School is not scary.
School is fun!

I can meet some
new friends.

Can I hear the story, too?

School is so much fun.
I am making lots of new friends.

The teacher is nice, too!

I think I'll come back tomorrow.